# Praise for Tw

"*Twice-Spent Comet* by Ziggy Schu[...] whimsy, hope, and unexpected magic in the unlikeliest of places. This fairy tale for the forgotten paints a breathtakingly beautiful story about Fer, a convict whose universe has shrunk to the confines of an asteroid, where they share space with other prisoners and lost hopes. But one magical moment changes everything—a mermaid, bathed in starlight, looks back at Fer, igniting a new spark in their otherwise bleak existence.... This story is both fantastical and deeply human, offering a reminder that even in the darkest places, magic and hope can find a way to break through.... A must read."
— **Cassandra Bivens, *Casla Reads***

"It's always impressive when an author manages to pack enough information into a novella that the reader isn't left feeling like something's missing or it should have been a longer book, and Ziggy Schutz has absolutely accomplished that with *Twice-Spent Comet*, a beautiful story about Fer, who yearns for belonging and to find a strong connection that can't be easily severed.... The book reads like a fairy tale, with just the right amount of seriousness mixed with magical wonder."
—**Elle, *Little Vermo Reviews***

"This was a gorgeous, heart-warming tale of losing and finding, of found family and beloved friends, and of how the absolute wrong things can lead to the absolute best. Plus, like, you know, space mermaids and shining-bright LGBTQ+ representation."
—**The Shayne-Train**

"If you enjoy well written LGBTQ+ representation set in the mysterious vastness of outer space—*Twice-Spent Comet* is a must-read for you!"
—**Jinx Isaacs, WatchfulEye.Art**

"A quick-to-read and captivating novella."
—**Jen Paul, Making Good Stories**

"Schutz crafted a beautiful story, which ties in the themes and the character arcs into a tidy package.... I highly recommend."
—**L. A. Lanquist, Trans Narrative**

# TWICE SPENT COMET

## ZIGGY SCHUTZ

Meerkat Press
Asheville

ISBN-13 978-1-946154-94-1  (Paperback)
ISBN-13 978-1-946154-95-8  (eBook)

Book cover and interior design by Tricia Reeks

Printed in the United States of America

Published in the United States of America by
Meerkat Press, LLC, Asheville, NC
www.meerkatpress.com

for all the comets in my life
who let me wish on them
as many times as i need to.

*In the beginning, before Humans had claimed the stars as their own, they held hands as they watched lights streak across the sky and called it Magic.*

*Magic, as everyone knows, must be Spoken and Heard and Believed, and so it was so, that stars were Magic, and those that fell especially so.*

*Sometimes, the beginnings of stories are just as simple as that.*

~~

Waking up is always the hardest part.

Fer's been on this rock long enough that they've gotten used to the routine. Even grown to almost like it. Maybe it is just like an earthborn kid, to search for the positives of the place that's going to kill you, but it's hardly the worst of the habits Fer was born into. On the days that feel just that much longer, they even take to listing those positives, counting them off on fingers that no longer swell with just one day's work.

They like how easy the work has gotten, when early on they'd barely been able to make it through the day. They like their new muscles, filling out fabric that had hung loose before. They're fed better here than they were in the prison or the transfer ship, and the companionship is a huge upgrade.

The transfer ship's captain wasn't a fan of lights for the

prisoners. Wasn't a fan of much chatter, either. And in the dark, people lose things. Faceless, silent shapes. That's what the prisoners became, on that ship. Fer paced their cell aimlessly, spilled ink on a blank page. Even now, months later, there are days where words sit heavy on their tongue. Like they're a limited resource, waiting to be wasted.

Waking up has always been a slow process for Fer. On bad days, they wake up on that ship. On the worst days, there's a moment where they forget they ever got caught at all. Where in the moment before they're properly awake they really do expect to see the cluttered walls of their last hideout—dangerously close to being a *home*. Back before Adrastea happened, and everything went tits-up.

Then they open their eyes to the soft curves of their small cell, and they remember they're here. Officially occupying the middle of nowhere, six months into a fifteen-year sentence they're not expected to survive. And everything presses down on them, like artificial gravity.

But, hey. Could be worse.

Fer reaches over, taps the speaker set into the wall so that it'll stop telling them to wake up. They step into their orange jumpsuit, garishly bright against the soft blues of the metal walls. With an underlayer that will glow even brighter in the event of a loss of light, the suit is "the height of prisoner-safety technology," according to the worker who had issued it to Fer. As if Fer wouldn't notice the fraying seams or dried blood staining the cuff of one of the five otherwise-identical suits.

They saved that one for days when they felt especially lucky. Or bitter.

Today, they're mostly feeling hungry.

They duck through their empty doorway—no doors here, no barricading yourself away, just a thin audio divider that always feels slimy when stepped through—and into the common room, letting the noise of the only other occupants on this asteroid roll over them.

The best thing about prison is other people. Who knew?

## 2

In any other story, this cast might be familiar. Their silhouettes might do well against a backdrop of fantasy, where magic has a cost that is fair, where the only life sentence is living. In another story, they may be the stuff of legends—a heavy sword in the hand of the taller woman, a commander's banner behind her. Her armor tarnished not because of losses in battle but because she wears her survival like a warning. The slight lady, bent not in exhaustion but in anticipation, some long lost royal bloodline rising in her like an omen, casting magic with hands too fast to see. The young man, short in stature but never in presence, charming folks with beautiful lies as he robs them of whatever they don't need, wearing a different face at every town but still managing to have everyone know his name.

In another story, there might even be a shadow behind them, a patch where the dark sits just a little more still. Fingers stained in ink, words used sparingly but every bit as sharp as their companions' blades.

But this is not that story, and there are no castles to protect, no revolution foretold. Only space, yearning and yawning. Only an asteroid, alone amongst the stars.

(There is still magic, though)

(There is always magic)

~~

"Looks like it's going to be another hot one," calls Moll. Her booming voice carries easily in the domed area that connects their rooms and serves as a common space. Bare but for a table and some chairs, shelving for knickknacks that none of them own, and the storage unit, tucked against one wall as best it can be, a large rectangular container in a round room.

"Not all of us grew up in weather too hot to breathe in, Moll. Would it kill ya to turn it down a notch or two?"

Benat's grumble goes cheerfully ignored.

Moll, as the tallest of the four, has claimed dominion over the temperature control—both inside and outside—for as long as Fer's been here. She keeps it just a little too hot for comfort, and they all complain like they're working off a script. But Fer also knows that Moll checks all of their outputs during their lunch break, and when they're in the red, she turns the heat down, gives their numbers that extra boost. Moll's the reason so few of them ever end the day with a deficit.

Moll had winked, the only time Fer had caught her at it. "Conditioning, love. Always nice to have an ace in the sleeve, right?"

Moll's got two—permanent aces traced in thick white ink against each dark forearm. Because she makes her own luck, whether with her large, surprisingly nimble fingers or the permanent buzz of a contraband tattoo gun, which she slides out of a hidden chamber in her prosthetic leg and can reassemble in under thirty seconds, if her bragging is to be believed.

They're all a little in love with her, and she knows it. Fer would bet another ten years on their sentence that Moll's never met a person who didn't fall for her in some way or another. She's just that kind of lady.

Benat groans again, slumped facedown on the table, breakfast ration turning less and less edible with every moment she leaves it untouched. The drawl that marks her as a Moon brat is even more pronounced when she's just waking up, almost incomprehensible if you're not used to picking the words apart from where they slur into each other.

The red sheen of the metal cuffs that mark her as a murderer are often the only solid lines of her figure.

(The rumor is that the cuffs—with colors for each crime—came from an Earth tradition, cutting the hands off of criminals. People say they can sever a wrist as easily as they can snap together and restrain. Fer's never seen it happen, but they believe it all the same.)

Benat has the dubious honor of being the most high-risk of them all.

She doesn't look dangerous, though. Most of the time she just looks tired, like her body's never adjusted to the pull of the prison's gravity, artificially altered to match the Earth's stronger weight rather than that of her own home. Her shock-blonde hair hasn't had much time to grow out from when they shaved it during her transfer, and it sticks up unevenly, always betraying her on the days she spends tossing and turning instead of sleeping, and her eyebrows are almost invisible against pale, freckled skin. The only color she has on her is the deep purple bags beneath each eye.

She looks young. *Too young for a life sentence*, Moll had muttered to Fer, when Benat had first arrived. Like either of them are much older than her. Like anyone deserves this.

Fer's wanted to ask Benat, in the quiet moments after a long day when the barriers between them all feel paper-thin, what she'd done to earn a murderer's mark. But it's hard to talk about why they're here when Mark is so fresh in all of their minds. He'd been a spitfire, chatterbox, talking too much and too loudly, until he'd paid for it with a cut safety line and a room that still sits empty.

It's best to talk about lighter things.

# 3

*Magic has many forms, passed from hand to hand until smooth.*
*Magic can be wonder, breathed from one mouth to another.*
*Magic can be a spark that feels like home in the eyes of a stranger.*
*Magic can be the breeze reminding the lonely that the world is*
*bigger than they know.*

*Magic is connection, common ground, two voices telling*
*the same story.*

*Magic is the space between.*

~~

"Hey, if you're not going to eat that—"

Benat's palm comes down, surprisingly fast, and smacks at the hand reaching for her food. But even at her most wide-awake, she'd be lucky to catch Rack, a foot shorter than Benat and faster than anyone Fer's ever seen. He swears he's famous in at least three systems, although Fer's never heard of him. His cuffs are dark green—*thief*—and his eyes match, mischievous and bright. His skin is the warm brown of living things, and when he breathes there's a faint whirring sound, like something inside him is more metal than flesh.

He's fond of saying his best heist was stealing himself a new set of lungs. This, Fer can believe.

And that's them. Worn bodies around a small table, breaking

metaphorical bread before the day's labors begin. Their prison is built to hold eight, but right now there's only the four of them. The four of them on their own little asteroid, completely indistinguishable from all the other asteroids in this belt except for the fact that this one is owned by a rich developer, one who thinks prison labor is so very in.

Every swing of the shovels adds blisters to their collections and value to some faceless entrepreneur's portfolio.

Back on the holding ship, before Fer's trial, and then on the transport, there'd been all sorts of folk. From all over. But there's certain prisons you can only be sent to if you're human.

See, other races have rules about isolation. The words they use to describe the prisons like this one would translate to "inhumane," except that other species' words for cruelty often sound awfully similar to "human."

There's still a year left of groundbreaking to do, as long as their little team's numbers stay steady. Then they'll send in the experts, get to building the luxury retreat homes, and their little pod, with its eight tiny bedroom-cells and its rickety chairs, will fold up and take off for the next asteroid, the next quota, until all of their bones break or until the timers on their cuffs run out and fall off and their time is considered served.

But for now, Benat has pulled herself up enough to eat her food, shoving the congealed meal into her mouth without breaking eye contact with Rack. It's not especially funny, but Fer catches Moll's fond eyeroll and laughs anyway.

If Fer shrinks their world to just this, the years ahead don't feel impossible.

Unfortunately, it's not long before the alarm sounds, and then they're grabbing their kits and heading out. The screens attached to their shovels project the grid, dictating which of them is working where today, who is planting atmosphere-establishing seeds and who is digging holes for swimming pools and survival bunkers or whatever else rich people put in their space-mansions. The assignments always feel just this side of arbitrary, and they're always spread out enough to be just out of sight of each other.

Out here, all Fer can hear is their own breathing, echoed back at them by the edge of their artificial atmosphere. It sits well above their head, pressing down on them, a constant reminder that it can disappear with the push of a button in a watchtower thousands of stars away.

Fer ducks their head, pushes those thoughts away like so much collected dust, and lets their shovel bite into the rock beneath them.

**4**

*Magic is the in-between. Between life and legend, myth and mortality.*

*It holds hands with science and together they play skip rope as they write the rules of the universe. Important rules, rules that even stars must bend to.*

*Rules like . . .*

*If Life comes from light, and stars from dust, then every blessed thing that exists is made of stardust, lit by its own existence.*

*However, there are some beings who are more star than most.*

*There always must be those who push the rules, pull at the edges of the universes until they shift, and become something entirely new.*

*Tails made of the sky, held up by magic—some of these beings swim between worlds. They were others once, small crawling creatures with names and curiosity too big for their fragile bones.*

*Many stories start with an ending, and theirs ended in an explosion, every moment of them suddenly everywhere. Ages passed before they could pull themselves together again, and when they did, their bodies were no longer large enough to hold all that they Knew.*

*So they left them behind.*

~~

Before, when Fer first arrived, they kept one eye on the sky. For debris from the asteroid field around them. For rescue, something their old friends had often hinted at and half planned, but never something they dared put down in writing. More prayer than anything concrete. For something to do, as rocks break to reveal more of the same, same.

It should be strange, how quickly the movement above their head faded into the background, like noise in the heart of a city. But Fer knows the rules now. No errant rocks will be allowed to hit them—the bubble that keeps their atmosphere stable sees to that, built for future rich residents. And no rescue will reach them, because even if any of their people were as lucky as Fer was, to avoid a traitor's sentence, they'd be scattered like smoke off a gun—too far away to ever find each other again.

After all, bodies just make martyrs. And no matter how strong a revolutionary heart is, it can't cheat the distance of deep space and hard labor.

So, Fer keeps their head down, most days, lets space bear down on the back of their neck as much as it likes. It's why they miss the creatures when they first fly by.

It's only when they feel the weight of eyes on them that they freeze, shovel half-buried in the rock, and look up.

The first sense Fer gets is *vast*.

The objects are large, like ships, but also stretch beyond what a space vessel encompasses—like they expand past what Fer can comprehend. Streaking across the horizon like comets, trails sparkling and alive with much more than dust.

Fer should have been terrified. But.

They had lived the first part of their life so unbearably grounded. They remember what it felt like, when they first saw the ship that would carry them away from the bits of living they'd managed to cling to. More than bolts and sails and thrust, it was freedom, and they knew no matter what the stars brought them, they would never see anything as beautiful as that.

And that had held true. Until this moment.

If Fer carried any religion in their heart, they might have thought they were angels. Humanoid but not, limbs stretched out like wings or judgment.

Fer should have been terrified, *but*.

Fer had grown up a dreamer, had relied on stories to fill their soul when there was nothing to fill their stomach, devoured each scrap of fable they could get their greedy hungry hands on. Beneath the shell of boredom and routine is someone who has always secretly hoped for *more*. It's how they got into the rebellion in the first place—a sense of wonder well-hidden and hard-won.

It's blooming now, deep between their ribs, because they recognize a myth when they see one.

"Mermaid," slips from their lips, like a penny in a wishing well, and the closest creature turns toward Fer, eyes twin moons against skin dark enough to have its own stars.

Once named, one could perhaps see where Fer is coming from. The creatures' bodies trail off like ellipses of stardust, unsubstantial and undulating them forward through space all the same. Certainly, with hair that shines like nebulas as it bounces around their heads, "mermaid" feels just as impossible as "angel" and just as true.

But this is not why Fer names them mermaids.

# 5

And so they swam through the stars, and knew of humans but knew none, until they happened upon a ring of space rock and bright eyes spotted them.

And the bright eyes, the scurrying creature, they knew nothing of space except how to live in it, and they knew nothing of tales but their endings, but they let the large bodies and the stardust caught up in their fins sweep them away for just a moment, and although they had lived two decades and change, they opened their mouth and a child's voice spilled out to call these celestial bodies mermaids.

And the Mermaids (for so as they were called, so then they were) paused, for the scurrying creature was as small as they were vast, and yet with a word had Named them, and therefore Changed them.

And the Leader, who swam at the front because she was most Curious of the lot, she looked down at the creature, and saw them to be Human, and in this seeing saw that she was No Longer the same. And that scared her, and delighted her, and in that moment she was both Named and Found.

And the Human (for that is what they were), who had always been Lost through their own design, looked into the Mermaid's eyes and saw themselves, and saw the stars, and saw a story.

*This story, they did not know the ending to. And that made them Curious, too.*

~~

Fer stares at the creature, and she stares back.

And everything in Fer's head, every doubt and every hard truth and every bit of lost hope, goes quiet.

They breathe in, and think of a storm on a distant moon, one that disrupted their sensors enough that when the raid came, no one was ready. Their little rebel crew, dashed on the rocks of a government that only wants one narrative told, paints and paper floating weightless like flotsam.

Since that moment, Fer's been living underwater, unable to shake the pressure in their chest.

They breathe out, and no bubbles escape, leading them to a distant surface. They breathe out, and nothing terrible happens at all.

So they take it one step further.

"H'llo," says Fer. Not the most inspiring of greetings, but words come slow to them even when not addressing an impossible thing.

The being stares, leans close enough that Fer could reach out and touch the creature's bare shoulder if they wanted to. For a moment, Fer feels a weight push down on them, and they lock their knees, stubborn until the end. They've never kneeled for anyone, never begged, never asked for an inch they hadn't fought to earn. They're not about to start now, even with such an auspicious audience as this.

And then the whole sky seems to pulse. Fer flinches, closes their eyes, and when they open them the pressure is gone, and the mermaid floats in front of them, shrunk down to Fer's height with proportions to match.

"Oh," the mermaid says, voice a soft rasp. "Talking out loud. Of course. Hello."

**6**

*Sometimes, the beginnings of stories are just as simple as that.*

~~

The other mermaids linger just long enough for the first one to gesture at them, fingers moving almost too fast to follow, delicate and firm. Fer's seen similar signs from some of the gangs they grew up around, kids speaking in a language no authority could parse, usual methods of silencing with sound dampeners or pinned tongues having no impact at all. Fer's group of rebels had a dialect of their own, although it was scraped together from across Earth and three moons, each of them bringing a few words to the table from what they'd picked up from their respective childhoods. Theirs was by no means a large vocabulary, which the mermaids' obviously is. They all seem to move at once, fluid and fluent in this language that is much more complete than some failed rebellion's codes.

Complete and strangely familiar—Fer doesn't know why these space beings would be using signs that resemble ones they saw back at home, but can pick out a few they recognize. It makes them homesick in a way that always sneaks up on them. Not for the planet, but for the press of people, for the feeling of being another face in a crowd, of not knowing the names of your neighbors but knowing they'll fight for you if the uniforms come a-calling.

Their own fingers are clumsy, but they still remember how to say hello.

The creature beams, smile stretching her face into something almost human. The signs flow from her hands like a riptide, pulling Fer in over their head.

"Sorry," says Fer out loud. Forgetting to hold their breath. "I don't know enough to follow."

The others are swimming away, blending in with the stars as they do, but her only movement is to reach out, rest strange, cold hands against Fer's half-signed second apology.

"You don't need to say sorry," she says. "I am the visitor who has come to your door. It's rare we spend time anywhere with enough air to speak out loud, that's all. I can speak like this fine. I just had to find my voice."

Fer's closed fist rests somewhere above their heart, and surely she can feel how hard it's hammering, because for all their camaraderie, the others don't touch Fer.

It's not something they always feared. There was no avoiding touch, in a planet as crowded as the one they grew up on. It's just that since they got caught, any brush of skin reminds them of what it feels like to have the family they built be torn away, even as desperate nails cling. It's just that since they sat alone, in cells and in the dark, touch hurts the same way sudden light does. Like their body isn't made for it anymore. Another thing that they'd lost, in that final raid.

The authorities had found them last, Fer and their closest friend, tucked into a supply cabinet. It was never going to be enough—they knew as soon as they were boarded that the only escape was through an airlock and out of reach of anyone, forever. Some must have fought, some must have run, but when they heard the heavy boots in the corridors, Quarter Jones had reached for them, and Fer had reached right back. Like children, hiding under blankets and still small enough to believe that will be enough, they pulled each other into the cramped closet and shut the door behind them. There they had sat in the dark, Quarter Jones curled around the printing press and Fer curled around her, scared breathing bouncing between them as they played at invisibility.

Fer wished they had been brave enough to talk. If they were going to be found either way, they could have made the most of those last few minutes with the person who meant more to them than a whole universe. They could have opened their mouth, ever the storyteller, and spun an ending for them. A fantasy, a failsafe, something that was as out of reach as safety, but still. Something they could have carried with them.

Instead, Fer sat in the silence, and when the door was kicked open, they couldn't even find enough breath to scream. Quarter Jones had, though. Had screamed and thrashed, and in that last moment, had let go of their precious printing press to instead reach for Fer. His long artist hands, grip tight enough for her nails to draw blood as the soldiers ripped them apart, were as close to an ending as either of them were to get.

Fer wishes they had left scars, but no such luck.

Somewhere between Mark's offered embrace and Moll's welcoming handshake, they must have done something— something to show that touch was not a thing they liked, not anymore. So, the other three, four, three again filled the space around them with words of encouragement instead, enough to tether Fer to them without putting that fear in their eyes again.

The mermaid doesn't know any of that, and she gives contact with ease, without expectation. When she pulls back her hand, Fer almost chases it with their own. They hadn't known. Hadn't known a simple touch could be so grounding.

"I'm Ophelia," says the mermaid, and again, Fer is thrown by how human the name is.

"Like the drowning girl?" they ask. They are one for collecting endings, after all.

"Like the moon," Ophelia responds, and there's not enough space for her voice to echo, but it does all the same.

Fer has never met a celestial body with a gravity quite like Ophelia's.

# 7

*Curiosity has its own current, its own pull, has been tugging at the hearts of those trapped on the ground since they learned to look up. Curiosity led metal into space and lent bravery to those who wanted to follow.*

*Curiosity burned bright in a human who dreamed of stars and mapped routes to them with numbers and years. And when it went wrong, and her and her companions were undone by overreaching, sent into the sky in pieces too scattered to count, curiosity is what brought her back together again, waking up among moons they would eventually take their names from, her and the others who had once been human but were now on their way to being something More.*

*It takes them a long time, to pull themselves together again, to find each other against this new backdrop of theirs, further than most had dreamed. But not her, no.*

*They find each other in the end, though. Because that's what happens to family, in stories like these.*

~

Ophelia echoes Fer's name back at them like it's something delightful, a new toy just for her. She floats around Fer as Fer gets back to work, because not even meeting a myth will get them out of their quota. She peppers them with questions on where they're from, what they did to get here, and Fer . . . tells her.

Not all at once, but in stuttered stops and starts, because Ophelia's eyes literally sparkle when Fer describes the simplest things.

"I've never been to the night markets of Pluto . . . What did it all smell like?"

"And what did his face look like when you said *that?*"

"Do you think you'll ever see them again? When you get out of here?"

Fer winces at that, their strike at a particularly stubborn rock skidding off and narrowly missing their foot instead. It's easier to accept a slow death sentence when you don't have to say it out loud.

"Even if I manage to live through my sentence, and they all do the same, I would have no idea where to start looking." Ophelia has been floating on her back a few feet above Fer's head, tail occasionally swishing to keep her there, her arm dangling almost low enough to brush at Fer's close-cropped hair. Fer's stuck somewhere between ducking away and hoping she reaches down to run her fingers through the fuzz.

(Of all of them, only Moll had managed to avoid a shaved head before being sent here. Benat was still sensitive over her loss, but Fer thinks they would like the shaved-head look, if they ever got the chance to choose it for themself. No more hiding, not in cupboards or behind a curtain of hair. Not enough time left on the clock for hiding.)

At this most recent admission though, Ophelia sits up.

"How long is your sentence here?"

"Fifteen years, at least," Fer says.

The air around Ophelia seems to stutter. Her form stretching large again for just a second before she pulls it back. How casually she takes up the horizon. How easily she gives it back.

"Fifteen years? For drawing some pictures?"

"For propaganda," Fer reminds her softly. Ophelia appears to be ageless, but she looks very young in this moment, outrage over something so obviously illegal betraying naivety or a disconnect with the times.

All at once Fer is exhausted. They don't want to explain the state of the worlds to this woman, mermaid though she may be. Doesn't want the pity, or the anger that is sure to boil over in her.

Fer's been there, let themselves be pulled to fury and action. And it lost them everything.

(They wouldn't change it for all the stars, those too-brief months. They had already known fear, known it their whole life. Being part of something bigger didn't mean more fear. It meant finally finding something that made the fear feel earned.)

"I should go back," Fer says, and doesn't look up, doesn't want to see the look Ophelia is giving them. "It's almost lunch."

They don't ask Ophelia if she'll be there when they get back, but they do take one last peek right before the curve of the asteroid puts her out of view.

She's on her back again, signing up at the sky. If there's anyone there to answer, Fer cannot see them. Maybe they don't need to see each other, their presences enough to send ripples through space that only another impossible thing could hear.

She's probably asking the rest where they've gone. They'd been headed on some kind of spiritual migration, as far as Fer can understand it. To a place green and overgrown enough to be completely out of Fer's reach.

Places like that, creatures like Ophelia, they're as far away as any fairy tale. It was a nice interlude, their conversation. A nice chance to catch their breath. But Fer has a story already.

They return to it for lunch, and fully expect the mermaid to be gone by the time they return.

**8**

*Once upon a time, there was a dome, and in it lived a family, strange and shattered and family all the same, shared labor and blisters easily substituted for shared bloodlines.*

*And this dome is where they were born, and where they would die.*

*That is how these stories are supposed to go.*

Fer walks into the common room and into the middle of a discussion. It's a relief, because Fer doesn't know how they're going to open their mouth and talk about anything but the mermaid they met this morning. Best to let the others set the topics and tone.

"Hey, Fer! What do you think? Love at first sight—real or nah?"

Benat, head down on the table like she drags herself through each day through sheer force of will, snorts. "With a face like yours, you'd better hope it is. No one's gonna want to look at your face twice."

Moll laughs hard enough to almost completely drown out Rack's indignant shout.

"Now, now, kids," Moll chastises. "No fighting during mealtimes." It would almost be convincing, if not for her face-splitting grin.

Rack sticks his tongue out at Benat, who reaches over to shove at him playfully before freezing. Instead, she drops her hands quickly out of sight underneath the table, and stares angrily at her plate.

There's an awkward beat. If the cuffs think they're being violent toward each other, they can deliver a nasty shock, and Benat's, in particular, are notoriously trigger happy.

Moll steamrolls over the silence before it gets stifling.

"Anyway, I can put this whole thing to bed." She winks at Fer, which means she's either about to tell an outrageous lie or an even more unbelievable truth. "Love at first sight is definitely real. I know, because I've felt it."

This is enough to get even Benat's eyes off of the table and onto Moll.

"Well?" says Rack, practically crawling over the table at the older woman. "You can't just say that and not tell us the story, Moll."

Moll shrugs, doles out their rations for the meal like love ain't no thing.

"I was around your age, Fer. Eighteen, twenty years back? Got myself in a bit of bad news, ended up crash landing on this farm."

"You fell in love with a farmer?" Benat asks, exhaustion forgotten in the face of breathless awe. Farmers are the richest of the rich, on her moon, if Fer is remembering right.

"Not your kind of farmers, Benat. Just the two of them, the land had been a wedding gift from someone's second uncle."

"The two of them?" Rack squeaks. For a shiprat, he's charmingly easy to scandalize.

Moll looks pointedly at his chair, and he climbs back into it, mutters thanks as she tosses a bowl his way.

"Yeah, give me a moment. Trying to tell this in order."

Fer snorts, because it had been something they'd complained

about, last time Moll had decided it was storytime. Sequence of events is not her strong point.

"So, there I am, staring up at the red sky through the giant hole in my little ship's roof, and then two hands reach down and grab both of mine. And even before I see them, I'm thinking, man, I've never felt as safe as I feel in this moment. And then I see them both, and . . . wow."

This isn't a lie, Fer realizes, watching their friend's face go soft. This is the truth, and it's something she obviously thinks about a lot, even with it being twenty years gone.

"Her name is Hadra, and their name is Tammy. Neither of them had ever been off-planet, and here I was, with my tattoos and my leg and my broken ship. I thought, of course they're interested in me, they've never seen anything like me. That's all this is. They just want to hear some good stories. Took a few months for it to really sink in, that what I'd felt in that first moment was something mutual.

"They called me their little fallen star; isn't that just the cutest thing? There I was, prickly and young and not sure if I believed in love at all, and then falling for two people at once. It was like some kid's bedtime story."

"So . . . what happened?" Benat's eyes have gone glassy, hand clenching and unclenching like it was never meant to be empty. Fer wonders who she's thinking of. Where they are now.

If they're thinking about her, too.

"We got married, obviously. Lived with them for a couple years, still visit as much as I can."

"What?" Rack's shouting again. "You're married?"

Moll shoots him a look and holds up her hands. "What do you think these are all for?"

One of the first things anyone looking at Moll will notice is the tattoos. Covering both arms, crawling up her neck to caress the left side of her face, all steady white lines that Fer knew she'd done herself, even though some of the angles seem almost impossible.

The pattern on Moll's fingers had always looked like just that—some abstract pattern. But as Moll wiggles her fingers with a purpose, the lines take on new meaning.

They're all rings, each one unique. There's at least one on every finger.

"Am I married, he asks," teases Moll, and Rack grabs at her hand to get a closer look.

Benat's staring again, and it takes a moment for Fer to identify the emotion in her eyes. It's hunger.

"You're married sixteen times?" Rack is impressed.

"Do they all know?" Fer asks. "Do they know you're here?"

"Can you give me one?" Benat's voice is soft steel, cutting through the comfortable atmosphere like she really is the deadliest thing in the room.

And Moll looks at her, sees how she looks more awake than any of them have ever seen her.

And she nods.

**9**

*There are many ways to be a wife.*

*Once upon a time there was a girl who wanted to try every one, who loved the world and whom the universe loved in return. And years later, when she deserted some idea of what made a man and became the lady that little girl had dreamed about, she remembered that love, remembered the wonder of a child's innocent wishes and learned to fight for them with bandages and blood in her teeth. A tourniquet of a lady, a one woman army of progressively prettier stitches and a bedside manner that cut through bullshit better than any scalpel.*

*The universe loved her, and she loved the universe in return. Found pieces of it in her lovers' eyes, in the checkerboard skin of her husband's breasts and her partner's infectious laughter. Collected them all like a tree collects rings, filling up the extra space inside of her like her ribcage was always meant to be a shield of sinew and steel.*

*The universe loves her. But the law ain't the universe, sweetheart. And the law caught her, and she laughed as she ran away, like she always had before.*

*Only, legs get tired after years of playing hide and seek. No matter how many times one oils the joints.*

*She was never going to be the fastest. Not the strongest,*

*neither. No, her ace up her sleeve has always been these clever fingers, this silver tongue. Has always been her understanding that the enemy is the house, no matter who's dealing her in.*

*So she marks her story on her own skin and counts the days until it's time to make her exit. Stacks the deck as much as she can, pockets whatever cards and coconspirators she comes across.*

*As far as lucky hands go, this asteroid might be her best yet. She's never really pictured herself as someone's sister before, but she's got space inside her still. So she stitches their stories up, as she inks lines into their bodies, like it's a given that this isn't where any of them will end.*

*And it won't be. She knows it, knows it like she knows the universe, knows it like she knows every one of her rings.*

*A wife's got promises to keep, after all.*

~~

Benat doesn't look away as Moll brings the needle to her skin, just bites her lip against the pain.

Moll doesn't question Benat's request. She'd pulled out her gun as soon as the younger girl had asked. Wondered aloud at a general shape until Benat had nodded sharply at one of the suggestions, and gotten to work. Now, she chatters, letting Benat's silence hide underneath her own cheer.

"I'm always open with them. It's an old Earth thing, even. A girl in every port, they used to say. And it's not like I love any of them less." She gets dreamy when she talks about them. Moll's always the most eye-catching thing in the room, but now she's positively stunning, love softening her edges and blurring her lines into something larger than life.

"I think I love them all better, the more people I fall for. And every single love feels different, exciting but also like coming home, every time."

"What if you don't?" Benat swallows, her voice shaking but her hand perfectly still. "Come home, I mean."

"It's always a risk. But they all know what I do for a living."

None of them actually know what that is. Her cuffs are black, which could mean a multitude of petty crimes. They would probably be blue, like Fer's, if she were here because of the ink. Sometimes Rack liked to guess, but Moll had never given so much as a hint.

"Anyway, we don't get to choose whether or not danger finds us. We're all just holding tight to rocks speeding through space, in the end." Moll pulls back, taps her gun against a part of her leg, comes away with fresh ink on the tip. "Ain't that right, Benat?"

Benat flinches, but Moll's solid grip holds the younger girl's hand steady.

"What's that supposed to mean?"

It's easy to relax around Moll. She's good with people. Fer didn't know she could wield that like a weapon until this moment, and now Benat is trapped, pinned by a needle and a promise, unable to dodge away from hard questions. Rack's eyes flicker to Fer's, the hesitation in them obvious.

*Should we stop this?*

Fer shrugs. *If it gets out of hand.* They're curious, too.

Moll continues like she's too focused on the tattoo to notice anything else. "I've seen your sentence. It's a hefty one. You don't strike me as someone who went out planning to be a mass murderer, and yet, here we are."

Benat ducks her head, like she's embarrassed. Not ashamed, not regretful. Just embarrassed, like she's been caught in a lie.

"And yet here we are," she echoes.

"Oh," says Fer, staring at the gun, as the buzz of it worms its way into their teeth. The sensation is familiar. Bittersweet. "I know that noise."

They had a little oven in the corner of their common room, back when they were part of a paper that called itself a revolution.

Turned it on when they were planning their more serious moves, ones that had to include dates, times, and locations. Just in case.

Moll's smiling, but her voice is soft and so, so gentle. "They can't hear a thing, Benat. It's all space junk and static on their end. You can tell us."

Benat's shoulders are caving in, curling in on herself like the only things holding her up are secrets.

No wonder she always looks so damn tired.

"I didn't plan it, or anything. It wasn't premeditated. But I wasn't just some victim in it either. I knew what I was doing."

"And what was that?" Fer speaks in a whisper out of habit. They've always been braver in whispers.

"They were taking people. Taking us *apart*, so people who could afford to would buy the parts they needed to live longer." Benat looks up, and is suddenly, startlingly present. A whole person, not one hint of what she usually let herself fade away into. "Did you know when you kill an organ thief, they charge you for the people their 'stock' could have saved too?"

She sits there, their resident murderer, anger burning away the fog that she usually hides in.

Fer thinks Benat might have been the best of them, once.

# 10

*Once upon a time, there was a messenger. "The fastest in the city," she would say, not a brag but a challenge she met every time.*

*Some might try to call what happened to her fate. She calls it bad luck, and tries to resist the instinct to reach for the talisman she used to wear, protection offered by a half-forgotten goddess.*

*She crashes, somewhere between one point and another, where she's not really anywhere at all. When she wakes up, it's to a man attempting to remove her arm.*

*Benat is the fastest, though. Fastest in the city, she would say, and that day she proved it in bloodied knuckles and desperation.*

*He's unconscious before he even knows she's awake.*

*He's dead before the last heart he stole has a chance to stop beating.*

*(Momentum does the rest.)*

*Word gets around, when the third body shows up. The papers call it a vendetta. The police call it a murder spree.*

*Benat calls it a routing, a cleansing fire, like the lady in red she would pray to when no one was looking. She leaves a trail of dead organ dealers in her wake, and when the authorities finally catch up to her, she pleads guilty to every charge.*

*She expects to die when she's sent to the highest security prison in the system. Instead . . .*

*Instead, she falls for an artist with a laugh like the future, and a sentence almost as long as her own.*

*This second crash, this falling. This is the one that Benat calls fate.*

~~

"She was the best thing in the entire system," Benat says, staring at the finished ring with something like longing. Rack is under the needle now, a starburst just starting to burn across his collarbone as Moll works. Really, they should be getting some sleep, because as much as they try to pretend this is a break for lunch, it's really more like a few spare hours between one shift and another. Their schedule is perfectly designed to make them never feel quite rested, wearing them down hour by hour, minute by minute. Not even the seconds are their own.

"Is that why they moved you?"

Fer is off to the side, watching the horizon past their doorway out of the corner of their eye.

Rack groans. "Man, if you're about to tell me the only thing I had to do to get away from y'all was pretend to fall in love with one of you, I woulda been out of here ages ago."

This pulls a rare laugh out of Benat, which makes Rack grin for all of ten seconds, until Moll's needle hits a particularly sensitive patch.

"No, no . . . We caught on to a murder plot some of the other prisoners had hatched. Um, for the two of us. So, we snitched. Think we even got a few years taken off of our sentences for it. I don't know. By the time I finished with the investigators, he was already gone, and I was sent here."

"What was their name?" Moll asks, always the bravest of them.

"Just he or she is fine," Benat corrects, and Moll nods, committing the set to memory. Fer feels their heart clench. Using she and he as the preferred pronoun sets isn't uncommon. Fer can't feel winded by some pronouns that rest a little close to home, just because they desperately miss the person who had first introduced them to the duality.

"And . . . this is going to sound silly, but I'd rather not say her name?"

"Even though it's just us that can hear you right now?" Rack asks, nodding at the gun as it buzzes away.

Benat pulls herself in, as small as her frame will allow, and stares at her new ring.

"I wished on a star for him to find her way back to me. I don't . . . If you say a wish out loud, it doesn't come true. And I used his name."

Rack laughs. "Is this more moony superstitions?"

"No," says Fer. "It's the same on Earth."

"And on a lot of planets I've visited, too," Moll adds, and pulls the gun away from his skin so she can flick his ear. "Not all of us are purely shiprats like you."

## 11

*Once upon a time, a boy was born in the cargo hold of a courier ship. A surprise child, born halfway between nowhere and the closest star. An unwanted child, who stopped growing before he should, whose body wasn't made to standard, and ships like this have no space for those who don't fit.*

*He wasn't supposed to be there, so he learned to be nowhere for long. Learned how to dance between decks. Never truly welcome, so never outstaying it. No one wanted him, but he didn't mind. He wanted enough all by himself. Filled his pockets and his patter with anything not bolted down. He wanted, and he took, and—*

*Once upon a time, his heart ran out of time before he was ready. But that's okay. He's a real boy, made of magic and wood, borrowed and blue and beating. They can call him a thief, they can call him a fake. He'll stand by what he told the coppers that caught him.*

*Can't steal something that's meant to be a part of him.*

*Can't break something that wasn't working before he swallowed it whole.*

*Here's the truth, he tells the judge, as sweet as a shiprat can be.*

*Once upon a time, a boy ran so fast he managed to restart a heart, and claim it as his own.*

*He hasn't slowed down since.*

~~

"I prefer untethered from all groundish wishwashery." Rack winks as he says it, which earns him another flick, followed up by the gun returning to his skin and shutting him up.

"It's beautiful," Fer says. "The ring. She's going to love it when he sees it."

Benat stands up, stretching as she reaches for her shovel. It's nearing the start of the second shift.

"Oh, he's never going to see it. It's for me, mostly."

Her walls are coming back now, and they may be shorter but they've got twice as many spikes as before.

"You didn't wish for her to . . . find you, then?"

"Well, yes. I did. But . . . I was lucky enough to meet him the one time. Finding her again? I can wish all I want, but I don't want to hold my breath, either. He wouldn't want me to."

"You could always keep wishing," Fer offers, thinking about how many stars they've tied the same hopes to.

"Wishing the same thing over and over again? Isn't that just the same as wishing on the same shooting star twice? No, that's no good."

"What's that supposed to mean?" Fer tries to keep the defensiveness out of their voice and doesn't quite succeed.

"You've never heard that? 'Don't waste a wish on a twice-spent comet'? It's why me and my siblings would always call dibs on the comets we saw."

Fer thinks back to when they were smaller, climbing onto the roof of their apartment building just to get some breathing room, sending up wishes as fast as they could at any blur in the sky.

"Guess that one is a moony thing," they say, and something twists in their chest. What a waste then, all the words they idly tied to stars as they worked, hardly daring to hope it would speed them toward an impossible reunion with the family they had gotten to choose.

No. Maybe that's how shooting stars work on Benat's moon. Maybe that's how they work for everyone else. But not Fer.

It's the only bit of hope they've allowed themself. It was the only hope they had when they were earthbound, staring at a sky they'd never touched. It's the only hope here, because they don't have to hold it in their heart, where it could wear down. They send it out, and let the wishes find their own gravitational pulls. Little pieces of them, so that even if none of their wishes ever come true, there's still a chance their artist will see the same comet, wherever he might be.

Fer collects endings. But shooting stars don't end, not really.

That's the whole *point*.

They walk out before the alarm signals that they have to. They don't even care.

# 12

*Once upon a time, there was a kid who dreamed of leaving the world behind.*

*They dreamed of many things, but they always come back to this—wishing the ground underneath them was less solid, wishing to be somewhere far, far away.*

~~

The mermaid is there when Fer gets back, and she's still the most beautiful thing Fer's ever seen.

"Do you know any stories?" Fer asks, because they're tired of thinking about real people, of things they can't reach.

"I know a few," says Ophelia. "I was a scientist, not a story-teller, but we all grow up with a few, don't we?"

Do they?

Fer has fought for every one they could find, and now here is this myth, offering them freely.

If they stare at Ophelia, they can see their own face reflected in her eyes, so they don't do that, because they're not sure if they believe in love at first sight, and they're not ready to change that right now.

"I'd love to hear them," Fer whispers. Ophelia is close enough to catch each word.

"Of course," she hums, and this time she does reach out, runs her fingers across Fer's scalp, smiling at the sensation of their cropped hair. "Most of them start with 'Once upon a time . . .'"

Everything feels possible when a story starts like that. Impossible rescues, love in every color, even happy endings.

Fer knows those are the most unlikely things of all. They'd collected endings like loose buttons when they were young. Fer remembers the endings like worry stones. Remembers the girls drowning, turning to foam, growing old.

Happy endings are just choosing to stop the story at the right time, Fer thinks.

Ophelia is very good at that.

## 13

*Once upon a time, there was a person who took to the stars like they took to the roofs of their city, who could run but never far enough to feel truly free, and so turned around and dug their heels into the proverbial sand (they've never felt real sand) and linked arms with a family found (they've never known any other kind) and they even held their ground. For a little while.*

~~

"How will you find them again?"

It's been three weeks since Ophelia first floated down into Fer's life, although it feels like it's been longer. Something is untangling in Fer, words that used to catch fall off their tongue freely now, sometimes spelled out by quick fingers as their vocabulary is rebuilt and expands.

"Who, my friends?" Ophelia smiles, and Fer smiles back. Sometimes, they think they will be found out by their bunkmates simply because of the new lines their face must have—all the smiling they seem to be doing.

"Yes, your friends." Fer says it out loud, but also signs it, because 'friends' out loud doesn't quite encompass everything the other mermaids mean to Ophelia, friends and family and a flock all fitting into something different altogether. "How do you find each other, when one of you decides to stick around somewhere for a while?"

Ophelia hums, and it makes Fer's bones vibrate, like even the building blocks that make them up on the smallest of scales are made to resonate with her voice.

"Well, no matter how far apart we are from each other, we'll never be as far as when we first got scattered. And we found each other then." She flicks her tail, and sparks shoot up. She gathers them in her hands like it's nothing, to hold space between your fingers. "Obe thinks it's because when we pulled ourselves together again, we all got a bit mixed up in each other. And it's hard to lose track of someone who is also a part of you."

"Wish that's how it worked for us normal folks too," Fer says.

Ophelia laughs, runs fingers still streaked in light along the planes of Fer's face.

"Nothing about you is normal," she whispers, so that even if someone were listening, they would not hear her. Like the air between them belongs to them alone, and not to some prison system's real estate. "If you sent your people a letter, I'm sure it would find them."

"A letter?" Fer asks, and Ophelia pulls them closer, snakes around them so that their back is flush against her front, and Fer—

The memory of that supply closet presses down on their chest any time people get too close. But even before their little rebellion got pulled apart, small spaces have always made Fer's breath catch. It might sound strange, coming from someone who ran away from a whole damn planet for a chance at a life in space, a life not known for having space to stretch out.

But even the biggest of space transports couldn't support people at the density that they lived in Fer's hometown. It's hard for steel ceilings to feel too close, when they get to breathe in air that is just for them.

Ophelia wrapping around them should bring them right

back to that closet, to their ration stamp-sized first apartment. But instead, it's like the warm presence gives Fer permission to breathe, deeper than they have since they were first found out.

It's like being hidden by their own miniature solar system, and Fer can't recall ever feeling so safe.

"Like this," Ophelia says, fingers wound with theirs. She brings their tangled hands toward Fer's face, and when she blows on them, her breath tickles Fer's ear.

"How will he know what I'm saying?"

"Say it. Spell it out if you have to." And Ophelia pulls their hands through a simple message, one more full of truths than Fer usually lets themself indulge in.

*I miss you. I'm okay but I'm far away. Follow this, if you can.*

"Like a message in a bottle," Ophelia says, and Fer stares as sparks make each word linger in the sky for a moment before disappearing into the starfield above them, and lets themself believe that somewhere, somehow, Quarter Jones will hear it.

Fer doesn't want Ophelia to let go.

"Show me again?" they ask, and Ophelia does.

# 14

Once upon a time there was an artist.

And she was clever, and he was kind, and she didn't care for how stories were supposed to go. He wielded her pens like a microphone, his questions like a sword. She grew up starving, not just for food or love or a home but for change, for a cause too large for him to wrap her delicate hands around, but it never stopped him from trying.

She took a marker to the makeup of the world, colored outside of the lines of his own histories until it was obvious which shades were missing.

And it didn't matter, that her hands sometimes shook. That his lines wobbled with the weight of it all, muscles that had never been made to last. Because imperfection is what they were all fighting for, really. The right to be imperfect and still dare to take up space.

So her brushstrokes found every gap in the armor of the government's propaganda machines, and he filled every one with color, brilliant color. Colors that promised more.

Magic must be Spoken, must be Heard.

And with a brush in hand, Quarter Jones was magic.

(and following behind her, Fer made sure every bit of that magic was captured on the pages of their paper. A few words, *a period at the end. A message in a bottle, and Fer supplied the cork.*

*And Fer believed, Believed, Believes.)*

*But not all stories get proper endings. Even those filled with Magic.*

*Fer collects endings, but Quarter Jones never cared for them. Too busy writing new beginnings.*

*So there is no ending, for Quarter Jones. One moment his nails are digging into Fer's wrists, and the next moment she is gone.*

*Sometimes, the endings of stories are just as simple as that.*

~~

"I wish I could see my file," Rack says, fidgeting as he tries to keep from scratching at the new ink spilling across his chest, joining with the healed sunbursts of his shoulder. Only Moll's sharp eyes stop him from picking at the stark lines. "I'm not even sure what I ended up getting charged with. Wasn't allowed at my own trial."

"Well, that tracks," Benat says. She hasn't embraced Moll's inks with quite the fervor that Rack has, but there's the beginnings of a sleeve stretching over one arm. With ink breaking skin, it's hard to tell it apart from the slightly different color of her other arm, lingering evidence of when she almost lost it.

"They musta taken one look at you and known you wouldn't be able to keep your mouth shut," Moll teases, and Rack shrugs, not denying it.

The loss of Mark is distant now, softened by months of growing closer and, in Fer's case, growing in love. They're comfortable in each other's presence and this tiny fake kingdom, where they're not free but they're also not struggling to eat each day.

None of them would go so far as to say they're happy to be here, but they're content. For now.

That in and of itself is dangerous, but no one is thinking about that right now.

**15**

*The trouble with only knowing endings is you don't always fight like you should, when you see your own coming.*

*The trouble with only knowing endings is that you're always half-expecting your own.*

~~

"They let me see my file," Fer says. They're using their nail to doodle designs on the table, planning for when they finally get their own Moll original. They're no artist, but they have an idea, shapes against an open sky. It's a work in progress. "I asked. I think they were hoping I'd fill in some gaps."

"And what did the good old authorities have to say about you, Fer?" Moll reaches over them, retraces a line, and Fer smiles at the suggestion.

"Not a lot. I was . . . I was hoping it would fill some gaps in for me too, honestly. No luck."

"What kind of gaps?" Benat wants to know. They've all gotten better at asking, this last little while.

Better at answering, too. The others have, at least.

Now is as good a time as any, for Fer to join them. So they bite back the instinct to change the subject, retreat, refuse to answer.

Sometimes, change is an intentional effort. One you've got to double down on to make stick, no matter how much it stings.

"I don't know anything about my parents," they hear themself say, as if from far away. The distance here is intentional, too. They can't own this, can't be inside themself while they talk about it. It will feel too real, like a second skin made of someone they no longer want to know. "I was hoping for a . . . birth certificate, a name. Something."

They don't meet anyone's gaze when they say it. It's somewhere between childish and selfish, and rolled eyes will hurt just as much as pity. But it builds all the same, the expectation that there's more to it, and the words trying to explain just spill out.

"It's more about roots. Belonging? I didn't really want to belong to Earth, but knowing there was at least some record of me existing, or of me coming from somewhere or someone . . . But it turns out that was one of the things they were hoping I would fill in, so. Well."

"It's not worth much," Benat says, going for comfort but falling a little short. "Roots like that usually just mean more people can hurt you."

Benat has siblings and mothers that cried when she left. She may not be willing to say her lover's name, but she traces the names of her family members on her tongue every morning and every night, like a moony nursery rhyme.

It's sweet, for Benat to say that roots aren't much.

It's sweet, but she's not much of a liar.

"Lotta people pay a lotta money to make those go away," says Rack. That's a fact, and Fer knows it, because Quarter Jones talked about rebirth and records going up in flames more than once. Talked about the act remaking like a true artist, carving out her own body from the scraps life had left him.

But Quarter Jones was always the brave one. That was the problem. Was supposed to be the solution too, up until it wasn't.

Moll, as always, cuts right to the point. Down to the bone.

"Some old piece of paper—or some file with your mugshot

on the front—none of those things will tell you who you are. You don't get any help figuring that one out, Fer. You gotta do it on your own."

Fer grimaces. "I know birth names don't mean anything. That they're more about what your parent hopes for you than anything that's supposed to last," they whisper, voice thin. "Just wanted a piece of a parent, I suppose. Or a past. Something real."

It's silly. A childlike thought, pulled from a bedtime story that wasn't even theirs. No name or origin would ever be enough to ground them, when everything gets to be too much. It won't help them feel more real, won't cut through the dark, let more air into their struggling lungs.

Fer likes their name. Scavenged it, like they've scavenged everything worth anything in their life. They don't mind who they've made themselves into, either. They just wish they knew how much they'd really changed, how much of them was still following the expectations of people who didn't even care enough to leave them with something to go by.

Moll snorts. Moll is always real, always solid. She carries a gun made for creation, and stands sturdy and true and like there's no other options than the present moment.

"Parental hopes or not, that paper can get awful hard to change. Lots of people would've loved an opportunity to not have to bother."

Moll's also not going to just let this go. She does this, picks at what hurts until they're forced to confront them. Fer has watched her do this to Rack and Benat both, but this is the first time the focus has been on them.

"I know that, Moll," Fer snaps, already feeling worn, weaker than they have in a long time and hating themself for it. A signal, stretched too far from the source. Lungs straining against air already gone stale.

"I'm one of those people," Moll says, and her tone is solid

ground. "I grew up with nothing much too, and when I found out who I thought I was supposed to be, I clung to it with everything I had. But a piece of paper and a want to do right by strangers who named me couldn't make me a good man. Or a man at all. The boy in those records never existed, as much as I wanted him to. The day I let him go was the first day I ever felt steady. What-ifs, doubts like that . . . they're prisons, Fer. They'll trap you as well as any isolated asteroid. Only, when we make our own prisons inside our heads, rescue from them is a lot harder."

If Fer had been paying attention, they might have seen Benat's eyes shift to Rack's at the word *rescue,* or how the air in the room got a little thicker with nerves. But Fer is too busy collapsing in on themselves, and they miss it all.

"Moll," they say, and they won't cry. They won't. "I didn't mean . . . I don't know. I don't know what I meant."

Moll pulls up a chair, sitting beside them and not saying anything at all. Fer slowly, so slowly, lets themself lean against her.

"For the record," she says, after enough time has passed for Fer's breathing to steady again. "I'm glad I'm trapped on this rock with you, Fer. If I had to be here, I'm glad it's you."

The way she puts emphasis on Fer's name does not go unnoticed, and Fer is so in love with this woman, this older, sister figure, and it makes them so angry, angrier than they've been in a long, long time. Because someone as large as Moll shouldn't be stuck somewhere as small as this.

"I'm going to bed," Fer says, and hopes Moll can hear the *thank you.*

"Sit here a bit longer," she says, and it sounds like *you're welcome.* It sounds like *any time.* It sounds like *love you, too.*

# 16

*For the first time since the sentence came down to hang around their wrists, they doubt it. They want to kick and scream and fight and wish, only they're not sure they remember how.*

*Once upon a time, there was someone who always knew this is where they would end up. Who knew each free step was borrowed time.*

*And now, the clock has struck midnight and then some, and they are finally realizing they want something else entirely.*

*Endings are their only constant. They wonder how long they've loathed their own.*

~~

"It's not fair," Fer growls, fists clenched. They've already gone and thrown their shovel. They could pick it up, but if they do they know they're just going to throw it again, or find a particularly sharp-looking rock and bring the shovel down over and over until the screen shatters and the metal warps.

And then they'll be in trouble, and for what? For nothing.

It's all for nothing.

"It isn't fair," Ophelia agrees, and if she were trying to comfort, all soft and calming, Fer would storm away from her too. But she's lit up like a city under siege, like moonlight against the sea, and Fer has never seen an ocean properly, but they know what it feels like—to have to be a siege engine to survive.

Ophelia is angry too. That's what makes Fer stay.

"They're just . . . they're so much bigger than this, Ophelia." Her name rolls off their tongue, and they wish they were brave enough to say it more, because whenever they do, Ophelia's star-kissed cheeks sparkle with comet trails. Blushing seems all too human for someone as magical as Ophelia, but when she does it, it loses any commonness and ascends to somewhere just shy of holy.

Every little line of her makes Fer ache for her more.

"Tell me about it," she says, and Fer does. Fer's told her every-thing, and taken every word Ophelia has told her in return like a gift. Every story is something to treasure, and Ophelia's stories tell of places Fer's never even heard of, worlds they'd never even known to imagine. Years and miles disappear when told in her soft tongue and sweeping hands.

How strange it must be, to not think of your life in years, to not have to worry about sentences that need serving and average life expectancy when your hands are weighed down by cuffs and circumstance. To mark life in the winding ways of fairy tales, where endings are vague and the heroes never run out of pages when they need just a little more time.

Fer's life is pale in comparison. Under Ophelia's bright eyes, they share it anyway.

Fer never thought this asteroid could make them feel like they could love again, but they can, they have been, they are.

"Benat really believes things can be good, she didn't have to fight but she did, and she's here as a murderer . . . But she saved so many lives, doing what she did, and she misses her partner so much, and she deserves the chance to find him. And Rack is so young and clever and he's stuck here running himself into the ground, and Moll is . . ." Fer brings their fists to their face, pressing knuckles against their eyes until their vision goes past black and into nothing, nothing. "Moll is carrying us all, she really is, and she doesn't even mind, because she's just that good, and she's absolutely stunning and strong and . . . and she deserves better than this. They all do."

Gentle hands pull their fists away, and Ophelia's thumb brushes at their pulse point, right above their cuff. The intimacy shoves all the air from Fer's lungs.

"You love them all a lot," she says, and there's something wry in her voice, something unfinished and raw. "Are you gonna tell her? Moll?"

"Tell Moll what?" Fer manages to get out, trying to breathe to the tempo of Ophelia's metronome touch.

"That you're in love with her."

"What?" Fer opens their eyes to Ophelia's face, gorgeous and hesitant. "I'm not, I don't . . . I mean, I do. Love her. But not the kind that needs a confession." It doesn't feel like enough, this feels like something important, something they need Ophelia to understand. "I'm not . . . in love with her. Not in the way you're thinking."

And now hesitation melts into something hopeful. "You're not?"

"No." And the shock at the misunderstanding is enough to spur them forward. It's not conscious thought, even. Just a fact, a foundation. "No, of course not. I'm in love with you."

Ophelia's careful grip goes tight around Fer's wrist, and her eyes blow wide.

"I thought . . ." Fer bites their lip, their own lack of discretion catching up to them. But it's too late to take back the words, so they keep moving forward. "I thought it was obvious."

For the first time since the day Ophelia arrived, she loosens her grip on the amount of space she takes up, her presence spinning off in every direction. She's not merely bigger; she's an explosion, she's a star being born, and for a moment, Fer is surrounded by a constellation of a girl, and every bright point is Ophelia, and every point is overflowing with love for them.

Fer blinks, overwhelmed, and when they open their eyes again, Ophelia is back to being Fer-sized in every way but her joy, her hands cradling Fer's own like every part of them is precious.

"I guess I'd forgotten what a human's love could look like." She leans in, rests her forehead against Fer's. "You shine so bright already, I hadn't noticed you were shining in my direction."

Fer wants to kiss her, but that's against the rules. Everyone knows that. People fool around in prison, but no kissing. Kissing gets you killed.

So, instead they lean into her, savor the feel of her against them, and they get so lost in the moment that they don't realize they've left the ground until they think to look down.

The ground is several feet below them, and Ophelia's blushing again.

"I'm sorry. I'm just really happy," she says, like that's something to apologize for.

"It's okay," Fer says, voice full of wonder. "You're okay."

Ophelia laughs, and her tail flashes, sending them spinning.

"May I have this dance?" she asks, and Fer nods, holds her tight as she leads them through the steps, a few feet and a thousand miles off the ground.

Fer has no idea how much time has passed when something tickles the back of their neck, and Ophelia pauses. She looks up, lets go of Fer with one hand so she can trace something in the air. If Fer looks hard enough, they think they can just make out the sparks.

"A message?"

She nods. "I . . . I have to go. But it will only be for a little while, okay? I'll come back." And then she scowls, and Fer is reminded again how strangely human she can appear, even when flying. "Obe's timing is always terribly inconvenient. But I'll be back as soon as I can. I promise."

And Fer, forgetting for just a moment what kind of story they're a part of, believes her.

# 17

*All they wanted, all they'd wished for, for so long, was to be someone.*

*And they were someone, oh they were Someone. Someone who could be loved, who could be wanted.*

*Someone who could be noticed.*

*They shone so bright.*

*Someone was bound to notice.*

~~

There are many ways to design a prison.

The classic kind is based around surveillance. Oppressive cells and eyes staring at you from the dark. It's tall walls and guards with interchangeable faces and matching clubs. Places like that, your whole day can be decided based on whether the guy on the other side of the door is in a good mood or not.

Folks who have only known the classics might look at a place like this asteroid and think that it's soft. What's a little manual labor, in exchange for a sky? One interrupted by guard towers or too-high walls.

It takes a little longer, for the danger of a place like this to sink in.

Here's the thing about this particular kind of imprisonment—it's all well and good to have your own space. To take a piss when you want to, to track your numbers and get fed and do your time.

To occasionally spend an afternoon dancing, instead of working. To fall in love.

But there's no one to argue your case with, no gray area, no pushing the line.

Fer had let themself get carried away. They'd fought for every one of their twenty-something years, and then they'd let themself have a moment where they . . . let go. Where they'd relaxed. Just for a moment.

If they'd been back in prison, or even in the transport ship, they might have been able to plead their case. To claim that the sensors had misfired. To explain that this was all some big mistake.

But out here, it's all automated. The cuffs couldn't have known that Fer had been too busy dancing to think of flying as an escape. The cuffs don't care. All they registered was that Fer had been somewhere they should not have been.

It takes three days. Three days of Fer adjusting to Ophelia being gone, of counting down until she was back. But days pass easier now, with the chatter and the buzz of the tattoo gun filling their breaks. With more teasing tugs at hair growing in and good-natured elbows in ribs as they fill their dome with the new level of comfort they've found in each other, the days don't leave Fer feeling as empty as they used to.

Waking up to the dark gets easier when there's less darkness in Fer's own eyes to stare back at it.

Ophelia had promised she'd be back, and Fer believes her as easily as they believe in suns and sayings. Who is Fer, to disagree with a mermaid? If Ophelia is the one to say it, Fer thinks they might believe in many impossible things.

They should have known better.

They know how these stories end.

It takes three days, and when it happens, the fact that they're surprised is its own separate hurt.

They're coming off a shift, picking at a callus on their hand as they follow Moll into the common room. Their arms are sore, but they almost like the way they take up space now. In a moment of true naivety, in the moment before impact, they're thinking about how much harder it will be, next time someone tries to pull them away from someone important.

Like some muscles are enough to change anything.

They go to follow Moll inside, and instead are brought up short. And as soon as they feel resistance, they know.

The invisible barrier that separates the inside from the outside refuses to let them through.

It's as simple as that.

Moll turns, sensing something's wrong in that way she always does. It's why she might live to see fifty. Might be the only one of them to, at this rate.

"Fer?" she says, and then sees them, hand pressed against what was, to her, just an empty doorway. Just an invisible line between 'in here' and 'out there.'

"No," she breathes, and Fer can't remember ever hearing her so quiet. "No, stop playing and get in here, Fer."

"I can't," they say, even though Moll already knows that.

"You can," she argues, and reaches through, grabbing Fer's wrist and giving it a tug. It doesn't work, of course— the same thing in Moll's cuffs that lets her pass through the invisible force field is what prevents Fer from following.

"But you didn't do anything," Rack says, eyes wide with panic. Either he's gotten faster, or Fer is already starting to dissociate in anticipation of what comes next. Their own brain already curling around their awareness in a too-late attempt to protect them. "You . . . you never do anything!"

"Doesn't really matter, does it." Fer doesn't let their voice crack with the fear they can feel tearing through their breastbone. They should have told them about Ophelia. About it all. "It's all automated. You know that."

Moll's grip tightens. "I'll hold on, then."

"Don't be stupid." Benat flinches—where did Benat come from—and Fer feels like they're already floating, gravity letting them go early. "All you'll do is freeze your fingers off."

"Shout, then." Moll's eyes are steel, as effective as any manacle, not letting Fer look away. "Yell for whoever you've been meeting with these past few months."

Of course, Moll knew. Fer doesn't know how she does it, but can't muster the energy to be surprised about this. If they let themselves be surprised, they might start screaming, and that will be unpleasant for everyone.

Making it easier for everyone feels like the least they can do.

"She's gone." Fer should have kissed her, probably. Taken the chance. They'd been cautious about all the wrong things, and now they're not even going to get a proper goodbye.

Moll shakes their hand, reminds them they still have limbs. Still here, for now. "Do something, at least! Don't let them kill you without a fight."

And through the fog and the distance, Fer gets it. Can see the fear in Moll's eyes now. Moll needs them to fight, knows it won't change a thing but needs to see them do it anyway.

Fer can't remember the last time they did something entirely for someone else. Even when they fought, last time, it was more for them than it was for Quarter Jones. He was always the braver of the two of them.

Fighting, not to any surface but simply for the sake of making waves. Not to any end, but because Moll asked. It's a nice final act, as far as final acts go.

"You're right, Moll." Fer tries for a smile. Somewhere, on a control pad a thousand lives away, a light is flashing, counting down. "You always are."

Moll nods once, and then lets go. Rack is crying, and behind them both, Benat offers a single wave before turning away.

Fer doesn't blame her one bit.

They hope she knows them well enough to know that.

Fer fills their lungs, trying not to number their breaths as they do it—*how many do I have left? Ten? Less?*—and cup their hands around their mouth, shouting for Ophelia. At first, it's just going through the motions, Moll and Rack's eyes heavy across their shoulders. But then, almost as if the individual components of their body are refusing to lay down even as their brain is already fuzzy with acceptance, their fingers start to trace the words.

They remember Ophelia's lessons. Remember how easy she made it sound, to send a message with no known end point. As they use a mix of Ophelia's own language and the scraps they remember from before, they imagine each word leading the next, like letters in a bottle. Maybe, if they're lucky, the words will float long after they are nothing but dust. Floating between the asteroids without a care, washing up on some distant, undiscovered planet.

It was always going to be a life sentence, this rock. Having an epitaph is more than they ever thought they'd get.

*Sorry,* say the letters, carved into the space between stars. *I was a criminal and a coward, and now we're both stardust, only I've gone and left myself behind.*

Fer doesn't get a chance to listen for any reply.

# 18

*Once upon a time, they'd written in the dirt, and then watched as the rain had washed it away, leaving no memory of their presence here.*

*Only stories with something to say get beginnings that leave marks.*

*The rest of them couldn't afford to waste words on pretty nothings.*

*Still, when their stomach was empty, they recited endings they'd stuffed into their pockets, and wondered at how big a life one must lead, to be remembered after you're gone.*

~~

For the first nineteen years of their life, Fer lived in a city stuffed into a postage stamp. They sat on rooftops and reached for a sky that promised them room to stretch their legs, to spread wings they knew they could build if just given the chance. They cheated and stole and ran every inch of that city ragged until their bones felt as worn as the streets they knew too well.

And it had worked. The first time they'd left the surface, smuggled away in a box smaller than their prison bed but bigger than any space they'd ever slept in before, they'd felt it. Felt gravity let go. It felt like finally breathing deep, like a high they hadn't known they'd been chasing until they caught it.

And now . . . They feel gravity loosening its grip on them, and for all the fear and all the dread, they can't help but feel stirring excitement too, because at least it's like this. At least they won't die with their feet on the ground.

They're a collector of endings.

They always knew how their story was going to go.

Their vision blurs as their body rises up, and the last thing they see are stars, stretching from horizon to horizon, as far as they can imagine.

Even now, dying amongst them, they can't help but love these stars. The one constant in their small, short life.

With their last breath, they wish on every last one.

(they've wished on them all before, but surely the stars will understand.

twice-spent by a life spent.

as far as endings go, it's not the worst one they've known)

## 19

*Every loving thing is made of Stardust.*

*Even humans, far from home.*

*Even messages, caught by Curious hands.*

*The Mermaid sees her Human's message, and thinks of the stories she learned, back when she too was human, and believed in endings. Remembers a young girl in her bed, begging her mother to read the story again, because maybe this time, everyone would get to live.*

*What use are comets, if one can't wish on them? What use are comets, if they cannot fly?*

*The Mermaid shoots across the sky, faster than she's ever imagined, and she feels her fellows giving her bits of themselves so that she can push even faster, and it may take years for them to collect all the parts of themselves, but they love her, and she loves them, and she loves a Human, who is delicate and dying.*

*Myths aren't supposed to fear death, but in this moment she does, oh she does.*

*The Mermaid reaches down, hands catching a body that is still home to a soul she knows like it's her own, although only just. The Mermaid reaches down, presses lips to lips and heart to heart, and she breathes all the space she knows into her Human's small form.*

*Every loving thing is made of stars. Nothing can change that. The Human is still Human; the Mermaid is not.*

*But now, the Human is also a little bit More. A little more like space. Constellations a little more clear.*

*The Human breathes, and the Mermaid breathes with them, and the Universe breathes with them all.*

*(There's one more star than there was, before)*

~~

It's always the hardest part.

Fer wakes up.

They wake up, and they don't want to open their eyes. Because until they open their eyes, they can be anywhere they want to be. They can be tucked away in the small room they shared with Quarter Jones, writing captions for her political cartoons, which in the dream are still circulating around the solar system but haven't led back to them yet—a voice of the revolution put to paper by a crew of clever hands who felt invincible. They can be dancing with Ophelia again. Weightless just for the joy of it, not tied to anything but each other.

This time there's no cuffs around their wrists when they lean in to kiss her.

Fer can be wherever they want to be, but only for a little while. So, they open their eyes to the gray curved walls of their bunk, of their cell, and they try to not let it get to them.

And then the memories of where they had been when they had closed their eyes last come rushing back, and they shoot up in bed, gasping.

"Woah there, careful!"

Moll is there to catch them when their body, weak from their brush with death, sways to the left as the world tilts. Her hands are familiar and very real. Moll is always the most real of them all, hardly ever even appears in their dreams. Moll is here, and Moll is real, which must mean this is real, too.

"You gave us quite a scare there, Fer." Moll is grinning. The telling off doesn't feel as sharp as it should. "Lucky for you, you fell for the fastest girl in the universe."

Fer blinks at Moll. Vertigo makes it impossible to focus. "What?"

"Your girl. Ophelia. She caught you. She's outside." Moll's ready for Fer's lunge, hands pushing them back down before they really register their decision to try to move. "And you can see her soon, don't worry. But give your body some time. It's been through a lot."

Fer wants to protest, but their words come to them slowly, like a half-remembered language. "I don't understand?"

Moll pulls back Fer's eyelids, checking their vision for . . . something. It's practiced, a familiarity that makes Fer freeze instead of following their instinct to flinch away. Still, she must see them tense. Her hand finds Fer's arm, comforting and holding in place all at once.

"Listen, I've worn a lot of hats, Fer. Lived a lot of lives. Used to be a field medic before everything else. I know what I'm doing. Promise."

Fer doesn't know how to respond to this casual touch, like all of the little walls they had built for themself are nothing more than cobwebs. ". . . Doc Moll?"

She chuckles, and Fer feels themself relaxing, still not sure exactly what happened but willing to trust in Moll's laughter. Willing to trust how steady her hands are as they flit over them.

If love at first sight can be real, if mermaids can exist, maybe casual first aid can be a love language, too.

"Sure. Doc Moll."

"Oh." Fer waves a hand weakly at her cuffs. They don't know how to thank her for the clear affection, the care in each gentle touch. They default to what they do know, and try not to think too hard as their head pounds. "Black for deserter."

That earns them a wink.

"Among other things."

". . . Tattoos?"

Sometimes, secrets aren't secrets at all. They're just stories, waiting for someone to notice them.

"Tell me, do you know what happens to doctors who are told the way they've been helping people ain't allowed no more?"

Fer manages a slow-motion shrug.

Moll grins. "They become tattoo artists. No one notices a tattoo shop that's got scalpels and a surgery in the back room." She pats Fer's cheek gently. "Also, they're a lot of fun. Anyway, sleep. Dream of weird space girls."

"Mermaids," Fer mutters, filters lost somewhere between here and unconsciousness.

"Damn. You're not wrong there. Wish you'd mentioned her earlier, honestly. Took me ages to sweet-talk her friend, and there you were on the other side of the asteroid, confessing your love already." As she talks, she's fussing with Fer's blankets, and now that they've allowed themself to ask questions, a thousand more buzz on their tongue. All the things they hadn't been brave enough to ask, before. All of the things they thought weren't theirs to know.

But the regulation mattress beneath them has never felt so comfortable. Moll is close enough that when she talks, Fer can feel the vibration of each word, but her voice still sounds like it's coming from three rooms away.

"Although, I suppose I could have said something too. It was my fault she wasn't here when you got floated, in a way. Hopefully the ship will make up for it."

"The ship?" Fer says. They think they say it. Maybe they just think it, just spell it with their hands. Moll should learn this language too. Her hands, adored and adorned as they are, would be beauty in motion.

Maybe they say all of that out loud, maybe that's why the last thing they hear is soft laughter. But already Fer is sinking down, back into the dark.

Only this time, it's a dark broken up by familiar stars.

# 20

*Once upon a time, there was an artist with a laugh like the future and an eye for getting there, and she waited for no ending, told his own story with each strike of her pencil, like every piece was a fire that could burn away all of the injustice in the world.*

*Some say artists are dreamers. Some say they make dreams.*

*When the Mermaids came a-calling, he pointed her stolen ship at their trail and followed.*

*This artist is a dreamer, and he trusts in her hands, firm on the wheel, to see those dreams through to truth.*

*True dreams don't have beginnings or endings, after all.*

~~

When Fer wakes up for the second time, there is no confusion.

They remember gravity letting go. They remember closing their eyes and opening them to air in their lungs and questions on their tongue.

They remember Moll, tucking them in.

They remember not ending.

"You awake, then?"

Rack is by their bed, trying to look bored instead of excited. A thief he may be, but he's no good as a liar.

Funny. Hardened criminals, the lot of them, but none of them able to lie worth a damn.

It is harder, though. To lie to family.

"I think so," Fer says, and gets a huge grin for their troubles.

"Excellent. I'm supposed to bring you outside, so I sure hope you can walk, because I ain't gonna carry you."

Fer can walk, although their legs feel too long to properly control. They lean on Rack as little as they can, but Rack is surprisingly strong for his size, and he gets them through the empty common room and outside with only a few moments of imbalance. And outside, Moll and Benat are there, waiting for them.

Before Fer can say anything, Benat is moving, wrapping her arms around them tight enough to make their chest ache. Rack joins in, and then Moll, and Fer's eyes sting.

They didn't think feeling this safe was possible for people like them.

More and more, they are learning to like being wrong.

"Your lady will be here soon, don't worry. She's just gone to meet the rest of them." That's Moll, answering questions Fer hasn't found the words to ask yet. "The field wouldn't let her inside our front door, so she's mostly been hovering by the windows and badgering us every five seconds to see how you were doing."

"It was cute," Benat assures them.

"We all like her, don't worry," Rack adds.

Fer nods, tries to wipe their tears on Benat's shoulder without anyone noticing.

It takes an embarrassingly long beat for Moll's words to fully register.

". . . meet the rest of them?"

Moll pulls away. "You probably don't remember; you were pretty out of it. But while you and your Ophelia were dancing, I met Obe, another . . . mermaid." She reaches out, ruffling Fer's hair. "Ever since you called them that, it's impossible to think of them as anything else. Clever little storyteller. Anyway, Ophelia had sent him to scout for a ship, and came back to let us know they'd found one." Fer can hear the teasing in Moll's voice without looking up. "He hadn't wanted to interrupt you two, so he reported to me instead."

Fer remembers Ophelia signing as the other mermaids floated away. Had she already been asking for a way to save them? How had she known?

Maybe love at first sight was something she believed in too.

There's a burst of movement beside them—it's Rack, waving his arms like he's bringing someone home.

"Look! They did it, they fucking did it!"

Above their heads, the asteroid belt and the stars are blotted out by the whole school of mermaids, all of their tails shooting off little sparkles of excitement. They're chattering, and Fer could probably follow along if they were trying, but they're too busy looking for Ophelia. It takes them a moment to find her, because her smaller body is easily lost amongst the larger mermaids, but she comes darting down to meet Fer with a speed that takes Fer's breath away, in all the right ways this time. She wraps herself around Fer so quickly that she sends them both spinning, so Fer can later blame the dizziness on this, rather than admit how much even just a simple embrace from Ophelia can undo them.

Fer was as good as dead not too long ago, but now they are alive, every piece of them, alive and lit up by the girl in their arms.

"I'm so sorry" is the first thing Ophelia says. Her eyes are wide. Now that Fer knows what drowning is like, they wouldn't mind if they fell into Ophelia's eyes and never came up for air.

It should scare them.

Fer can't find the energy in them to muster up any fear.

"For what?" Fer says, genuinely confused as to what in the universe she could be apologizing for.

"For leaving you," Ophelia whispers, and oh.

No one's ever apologized for leaving before.

"But you came back." Before they can overthink it, they

lean in, killing the distance between them to press their lips to Ophelia's cheek. "You came back."

Beside them, another myth is chatting with Moll, one hand lingering on her arm, and Fer would tease her about needing a new ring but they know Moll will just turn it back around on them, and they're not ready to admit out loud that if they could they would marry Ophelia right here and now.

"I brought you a ship," Ophelia whispers against Fer's cheek. "And someone who can get the cuffs off too." Her voice goes soft, shy. "You don't owe me anything, but I'd like to come with you, if you want. Even if you don't, I don't regret asking them to find you one. You're the brightest thing I've seen in a long time. I couldn't leave you here in the dark."

Fer isn't the best with words. They'll have to find the right ones to thank Ophelia eventually, but they hope this will fill the gaps until they do, as they cup her face in their hands and kiss her, the way they've been wanting to for months.

By the little gasp and the way Ophelia leans in, she understands.

Above their heads, the sky opens, the mermaids all flipping their tails and signing their excitement. And through the gap in their wake flies their salvation—a vessel like a ship graveyard come to life, parts mixed and matched to find poetry in the construction. Almost impossibly full of color, after so much gray rock.

Color that's found the cracks in these old parts and made them shine.

"Benat," says Rack, tugging on the taller girl's sleeve. "Is that . . . you?"

Painted across one of the sides, like the plane skeleton Fer found once in a junkyard, is a pinup of a girl. She's got cropped shock-white hair and a smile that won't stop, and she is unmistakably Benat, down to the line of mismatched color between shoulder and saved arm.

Benat sucks in a deep, shuddering breath, and Fer recognizes the sound. It's the sound of someone whose lungs haven't been full for far too long.

"It's her," she says, not a drop of doubt in her tone. "It's . . . that's my partner's ship. It's gotta be."

And the universe is surely a strange one, because Fer knows this art. Knows it as well as they know their own handwriting, built a revolution with this art as the face.

All this time, Fer has let themselves believe their life is a tragedy. It isn't until the ship touches down that they realize this simply isn't true.

The door opens, and Quarter Jones steps out.

He tilts her head, and it's like the first time they met, Fer a stowaway, him the captain who took one look at the ragged person in front of her and offered Fer a hand and a family and a cause, all at once.

Benat is already moving, hands outstretched like she's in a trance, and Quarter Jones's hands come out to catch her and Fer knows exactly what that feels like. To need touch to believe, because Quarter Jones is made of impossible things.

"Hey, Fer." Her voice is clear and cutting and warm like home. Then to Benat, "Hey, babe. See you've met the in-laws already. Always knew you two would get along."

Once upon a time, in a closet on a ship being boarded by an enemy too big to fight, an artist had taken out a knife and cut across his palm, her voice whispering a promise. Fer had copied the line across their own skin, clasped their hands together with the closest thing to blood they had ever known.

"We're siblings, Fer," said Quarter. "They can't take that away from us."

And Fer, Fer knows endings. Knew endings. Had learned, through the months of adding pointed words to Quarter Jones' art, that a few words could make something true when said at the right time.

"We'll find each other again," they said. A role reversal, hope strange on their tongue while their impossible best friend lets himself grieve everything they're all losing, with each new step of the soldiers' boots outside their hiding place.

Quarter Jones hadn't believed them then, and Quarter Jones had taught Fer so much about belief. It was the least they could do, to hold this torch for her. And Fer can see the gratitude in his eyes now, like this was all somehow Fer's doing, this chance meeting, this fairy-tale rescue.

They hold Ophelia's hand tight, and reach out with the other, letting their sibling pull them onto her ship and into another story altogether.

Fer doesn't know this ending.

Against a field of stars bright enough to block out any lingering dark, it doesn't scare them like it should.

**21**

*Once upon a time, there was magic.*

*There still is, if you know where to look. If you learn to catch it, like stars moving in the corner of your eyes.*

*Magic has a way of making everything feel closer. Magic is what makes the sky close enough to touch, if you reach out often enough. Magic is connection out of nothing, tying strangers into a family tree. Magic is making space feel vast and at the same time so, so small.*

*And sometimes, just sometimes, Magic is wishing twice on a falling star.*

# Acknowledgments

Like with any terraformed asteroid or revolution, it takes a found family, and I have been surrounded by an amazing one while writing this. Thank you to the Hostel, for making sure I always have a place to come home to. Thank you to my partners, who hold my heart with as much care as any starfield. And thank you to family both born and found, for always encouraging my words, spoken or written, hard won or easily given.

Thank you to Meerkat, who eight years ago gave me my first "yes" and then celebrated every additional "yes" I got. I'm so glad my first longer piece gets to be with you, too.

And thank you to the communities who hold me up. To my queer siblings, my disabled siblings, to the other previvors who help me be strong just by being strong themselves. Again and again you offer soft places to land, even when it feels like all I know is falling.

Thank you to everyone who believes in me. You are the constellations I wish on every time I sit down to tell a story.

And thanks to you, reader. Even just by holding this book in your hands, you're helping make a dream I've had since I was eight years old come true.

# About the Author

Ziggy Schutz (she/him/he/her) is a queer, disabled, proud previvor mess who is at all times looking for ways to make his favorite fairytales and horror stories reflect people who look a little more like her.

Ziggy is the writer and creator of Crossing Wires, a hopeful post-apocalyptic podcast, as well as having over 25 short stories and such published. Twice-Spent Comet is his first published longer work.

For more of her writing, visit linktr.ee/ziggyschutz.

photo credit: Katelsize Dubbs

## DID YOU ENJOY THIS BOOK?

If so, word-of-mouth recommendations and online reviews are critical to the success of any book, so we hope you'll tell your friends about it and consider leaving a review at your favorite bookseller's or library's website.

Visit us at www.meerkatpress.com for our full catalog.

Meerkat Press
Asheville

Printed in the USA
CPSIA information can be obtained
at www.ICGtesting.com
LVHW041405221124
797179LV00005B/102

* 9 7 8 1 9 4 6 1 5 4 9 4 1 *